The
Fog Boggarts

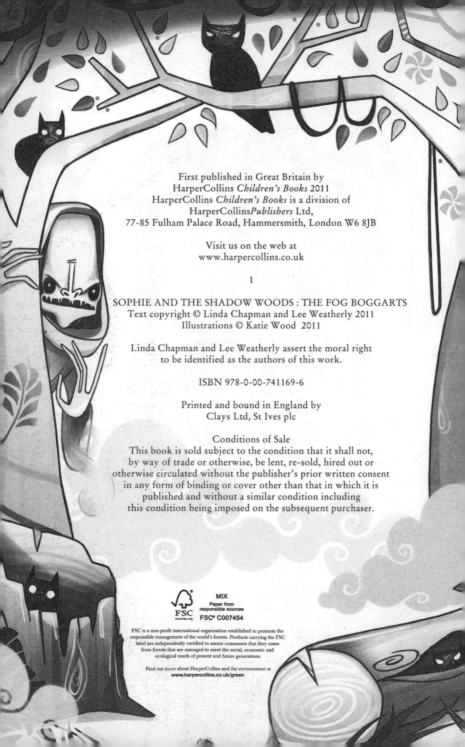

First published in Great Britain by
HarperCollins *Children's Books* 2011
HarperCollins *Children's Books* is a division of
HarperCollins*Publishers* Ltd,
77-85 Fulham Palace Road, Hammersmith, London W6 8JB

Visit us on the web at
www.harpercollins.co.uk

1

SOPHIE AND THE SHADOW WOODS : THE FOG BOGGARTS
Text copyright © Linda Chapman and Lee Weatherly 2011
Illustrations © Katie Wood 2011

Linda Chapman and Lee Weatherly assert the moral right
to be identified as the authors of this work.

ISBN 978-0-00-741169-6

Printed and bound in England by
Clays Ltd, St Ives plc

MIX
Paper from
responsible sources
FSC® C007454
www.fsc.org

FSC is a non-profit international organisation established to promote the
responsible management of the world's forests. Products carrying the FSC
label are independently certified to assure consumers that they come
from forests that are managed to meet the social, economic and
ecological needs of present and future generations.

Find out more about HarperCollins and the environment at
www.harpercollins.co.uk/green

More

Sophie
AND THE
Shadow Woods

adventures:

The Goblin King
The Swamp Boggles
The Spider Gnomes

Linda Chapman & Lee Weatherly

The Fog Boggarts

Illustrated by Katie Wood

HarperCollins *Children's Books*

To Iola and Charlotte for all the wonderful suggestions you make about the shadow creatures. Thank you!

Contents

The Shadow Woods...

Very few people ever enter the Shadow Woods. The crooked trees press closely together, their branches reaching out like skeletons' arms. Strange whispers echo through the quiet air, and eyes seem to watch from the shadows. Anyone who does go in soon leaves, their skin prickling with fear. For these woods are like no others. Hidden deep within them is a gateway to the Shadow Realm – a dark and chaotic world where all the mischief-making creatures like goblins, boggles and trolls live.

Many hundreds of years ago, the Shadow Realm

creatures could pass freely between our world and theirs, but they caused so much trouble that it was decided the gateway between the two worlds must be shut for good. Yet no one knew how to do this, until a locksmith with magical powers made an iron key and then slotted a gem from the Shadow Realm into its handle. The secret had been found! The locksmith forced as many shadow creatures as he could back into their own world and locked the gateway firmly behind them.

From that day on, the locksmith became the Guardian of the Gateway, watching over the precious key and stopping the few shadow creatures left in this world from causing too much trouble. As he grew old he passed his powers on

to his grandson, who in turn passed the powers on to his. For hundreds of years, the Guardianship has passed down from grandparent to grandchild, and the gate has always remained safely shut.

But now for the first time, disaster looms. The shadow creatures have stolen the iron key! Luckily, there was no gem in its handle when it was taken, but there are six gems from the Shadow Realm hidden somewhere in our world. If the shadow creatures find any of them, they'll be able to slot them into the key and open the gateway, letting hordes of villainous creatures loose to cause mayhem and trouble.

Only one girl stands in their way... and her name is Sophie Smith.

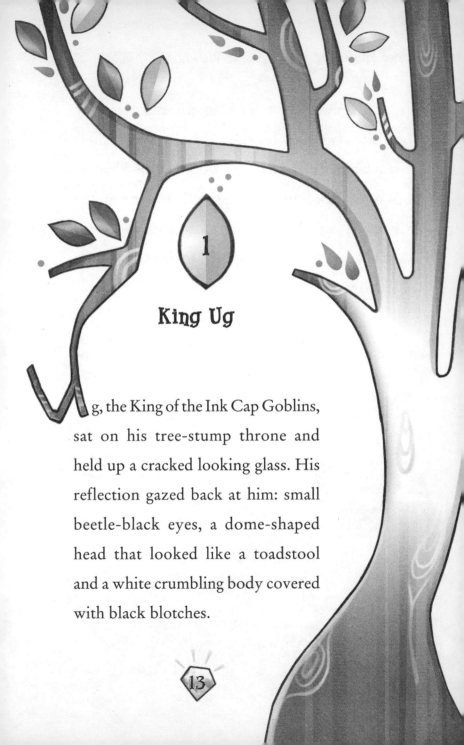

1

King Ug

Ug, the King of the Ink Cap Goblins, sat on his tree-stump throne and held up a cracked looking glass. His reflection gazed back at him: small beetle-black eyes, a dome-shaped head that looked like a toadstool and a white crumbling body covered with black blotches.

Ug smirked. "Oh, yes!" he crooned, tweaking a flake of skin off his chin. "I really am the most handsome creature in the whole of the Shadow Woods. *And* the bravest. When I open the gateway, all the other shadow creatures shall be proud to call me king. All I need is one little shadow gem."

He touched the iron key that hung around his neck on a rope and frowned. There had once been six hidden shadow gems but the new Guardian – a mere girl – had already found three of them. He *had* to find one of the others!

Jumping off his throne, King Ug strode to the edge of the clearing. "Where are those useless servants of mine?" he muttered. "Have they done what I asked?" He opened his mouth to yell, but just then three other Ink Cap Goblins came running up. One had a knobbly nose like a potato, one had massive feet and one had particularly crumbly skin. Skidding to a stop in front of Ug, they all started to bow.

"We're back, oh Great King Ug," panted Potato Nose, bobbing up and down.

"We're here!" exclaimed Flaky Face.

"We've returned!" said Big Feet.

Ug rolled his eyes. "I'm not blind. I can see that! So? Did you find the Fog Boggarts's caves? Will they help us?"

The goblins in front of him exchanged nervous looks.

"We did find the caves…" Flaky Face began cautiously.

"And we *did* speak to the Fog Boggarts," put in Potato Nose.

"But they… um… they…" Big Feet looked anxious.

Ug frowned. "They *what?*"

The words came out of Big Feet in a rush. "They said they wouldn't speak to servants and that they wanted to talk to you themselves! They're coming here right now."

Ug's white face went even paler. "What? The most dangerous shadow creatures in the woods

– creatures who can open their mouths so wide they can swallow a person in one gulp – are coming here? To talk to *me? Right now?*"

Big Feet nodded.

"Ah – right," said King Ug finally. He chewed his finger nervously, his black, beady eyes darting to the trees around them. "Well, that's fine. Yes, indeed, looking forward to seeing them. Though maybe I'll just – take a little stroll first..." He edged towards the trees, but it was too late. Thick grey fog was already creeping in on all sides, blocking his way.

"Erp," squeaked Ug. The other goblins gulped as the fog surrounded them. Before their eyes, a shiver ran through the white mist. Suddenly ten tall, thin creatures were standing there. Their skin was grey and their eyes were like large, dark holes in their long faces. Their

mouths stretched almost from one ear to the other. Ug stood up straight and managed a sickly smile of greeting.

One of the creatures stepped forwards, wearing a raggedy dress. Her voice was a sinister

whisper. "King Ug, I am Spindle Fingers, Queen
of the Fog Boggarts."

Ug inclined his head. "Greetings, Your Most
Majestical Majesty."

Spindle Fingers bowed back, and then her

eyes narrowed. "Your servants came to find us, King Ug. They told us you wanted our help with the little matter of finding a shadow gem. Is this true?"

Ug attempted a confident chuckle. It sounded more like a nervous cough. "Oh, that. Well, only if it's quite convenient. I mean…" He shuddered, catching sight of the queen's gaping mouth. "Yes, Your Majesty."

Her dark gaze bored into him. "May I see *the key*?"

Trying to hide his shaking fingers, Ug took the key from around his neck and held it out. A whisper ran round the circle of Fog Boggarts.

"The key that can unlock the gateway," Spindle Fingers breathed.

Ug pointed to a hole in the handle. "But – but only if a shadow gem is fitted in here. Without a

shadow gem it won't work. And there are only three gems still hidden."

Queen Spindle Fingers's eyes gleamed. "Ah, but the key glows when it is near a gem! We shall search all of the human world until we find where one is hidden." Moving forwards, she whipped the key out of Ug's hands. "We Fog Boggarts have many tricks up our sleeves we can use. If one way doesn't work, there are others."

With a ripple, she changed to a human form, taking on the shape of a pretty woman with shoulder-length blonde hair.

She simpered at the group. "Between this and our other powers, those pitiful humans won't know what's hit them! We shall

find a gem, open the gateway and all shadow creatures will bow before the Fog Boggarts."

A hissing laugh ran round the group. Spindle Fingers smiled evilly, stroking the key, and then dissolved into the mist. One by one, the other Fog Boggarts followed after her, until none were left.

There was silence.

"You idiots!" burst out King Ug, wheeling on the three Ink Cap Goblins. "You are my guards. You're supposed to *guard* me! Now the Fog Boggarts have the key!"

"Maybe they'll bring it back with a gem," said Flaky Face hopefully.

Ug glared at him. "They most certainly will, because *you* will make sure of it."

Flaky Face's mouth fell open. "Me?" he squeaked.

"Yes, you! Follow them – don't let that key out of your sight! When they find the gem, make sure they bring it here. And if they don't, steal it!"

"Steal it?" quavered Flaky Face. "From the Fog Boggarts?"

The other two goblin servants sniggered.

Ug turned on them. "I don't know what *you're* laughing at. You're both going too!" He cuffed them around the ears. "Now follow that key and don't come back without it!"

Picking up some pine cones, he started throwing them at the trio. They ran from the clearing, howling as the hard missiles bounced off their soft white heads.

Marching back to his throne, Ug threw himself down. For a moment, he sat scowling, but then his face began to crease into a smile. If anyone could find a shadow gem, it surely *had* to be the Fog Boggarts. As Ug thought about the Fog Boggarts sneaking their way into the town of Upper Gately, his smile grew even wider. That pesky girl Guardian wouldn't stand a chance against the Fog Boggarts. No, not a single chance…

2

Going Exploring!

Sophie and Sam stood in front of the kitchen window. A grey parrot was sitting on the curtain rail, watching them. "Hello, Nigel," Sam said.

The grey parrot cocked his head to one side. "Hello, Nigel."

"No, you should say hello to me – say 'Hello, Sam'," Sam told him.

His spiky red hair stood almost straight up from his head. Nigel seemed to be eyeing it.

"Strawberry jam!" he squawked, flapping his wings.

Sophie and Sam giggled. Nigel the parrot was staying at Sophie's house while his owner was on holiday. Sophie loved him – not only was he

funny when he said things wrong, but he had also proved to be very useful the last time she and Sam had been fighting the shadow creatures.

Just then, the kitchen door opened and Mrs B, the housekeeper, came in. Her cheeks were pink and her grey hair was escaping from its bun. Sophie's parents were archaeologists, and often had to go abroad to work. When they were away from home like now, Sophie's grandfather moved in, and he and Mrs B looked after Sophie and her twin brother, Anthony.

"Hello, you two," said Mrs B, putting her shopping down. "What are you doing?"

"Just going out to play in the garden," said Sophie quickly. She kept her expression innocent. It would never do for Mrs B to suspect what she and Sam were really hoping to do!

"Okey-dokey." Mrs B looked up at the parrot.

"Now, I've got tea to get ready, so time to get back in your cage now, Nigel. Down you come!"

"BUM!" shrieked Nigel, throwing his head back as he screeched the word.

Sophie and Sam burst out laughing. Mrs B gave an embarrassed chuckle as Nigel flew down and landed on her shoulder. "Oh, Nigel, what are you like!"

He rubbed his head against her cheek. "Bum!" he told her happily.

Still giggling, Sophie and Sam went out of the back door. But their mood grew more serious as they gazed at the dark woods at the bottom of Sophie's garden.

"You're really sure about this plan of going into the Shadow Woods to explore?" Sam questioned.

Sophie nodded. "Yes! We haven't seen any

shadow creatures all week and I bet King Ug's planning something. He's not going to give up on finding the three remaining gems. If we go into the woods we might discover what he's up to. Of course, you don't have to come with me," she teased as they reached the fence at the bottom of her garden. "You can stay here and help Mrs B and Nigel cook tea, and I'll have an adventure on my own and—"

Sam threw himself over the fence. "Last one into the woods is an Ink Cap Goblin!"

Sophie scrambled after him. Grinning at each other, they ran into the darkness of the trees.

Two weeks ago there was no way Sophie would have thought about exploring the Shadow Woods, but that was before she found out that she was the Guardian of the Gateway. Her grandfather, the old Guardian, had explained that she had to make sure the gateway was always kept locked. Unfortunately, on the day before Sophie had become Guardian, one of the shadow creatures, King Ug, had managed to steal the key and now he was trying to open the gateway himself. Sophie was determined to stop him and get the key back!

The track twisted and turned. Brambles snagged at Sophie's jeans and trainers and leaves caught in her long blonde ponytail. The branches were thick overhead and there wasn't much light. Sam got out his new super-bright wind-up torch and turned it on. The beam dazzled out.

"Don't you think it was really clever of someone to invent a torch like this?" he said, examining it. "You just wind the handle and the battery recharges." Sam loved science and was very brainy. "You see, winding the handle

creates kinetic energy," he said, as Sophie shook her head. "Which goes into the battery where it changes to electrical energy and…"

Sophie held back a groan. "Too much info! I prefer *this* kind of energy!" Running forwards, she jumped into the air and kicked out with her feet, one after the other. Sophie was good at all sports, but particularly loved tae kwon do. One of the best things about being the Guardian was having a chance to use tae kwon do for real.

"Hi-YA!" she cried, pretending there was a shadow creature behind her.

She stopped with a gasp as her toes started to tingle. Whenever she was near to a shadow creature, the Guardian magic made her super-strong and super-fast. It always started as a tingling feeling in her feet. Just like this!

"What's up?" said Sam, seeing her face.

"There must be some shadow creatures nearby!" Sophie whispered. "I can feel my powers starting to work." She raced along the path, jumping over tree roots and pushing aside branches.

"Sophie! Wait!" Sam had to sprint to catch up with her. She could go much faster than him when her powers kicked in.

Sophie slowed down a bit, but excitement was churning through her. Her Guardian powers always made her feel very brave. "What's that

noise?" she asked, hearing a low roaring sound through the trees.

Sam frowned. "It almost sounds like a waterfall."

"It *is* a *waterfall*!" said Sophie in astonishment as they emerged through the trees. There was a craggy grey cliff, with water cascading over the top of it into a river below.

"Weird!" said Sam, turning off his torch. "I didn't even know there *was* a waterfall in these woods."

Sophie shook her head, lost for words. The exploring they had done in the Shadow Woods had made her realise they were very strange indeed – they never seemed quite the same from one day to the next. Suddenly she noticed something else.

"Look!" She pointed to the base of the cliff

where there were some shadowy caves, their entrances like dark doorways. "They look like just the sort of place a shadow creature might live. Come on, let's go and check it out!"

Sam stared uncertainly at the dark opening. "Or we could just walk on by. I bet it's a quiet and polite shadow creature, staying out of trouble, doing its own thing…" His voice trailed off as Sophie strode off towards the caves, her blonde ponytail swinging. "Oh, why do I bother?" he said, rolling his eyes and hurrying after her.

Sophie had reached the entrance to the first cave. As she stepped inside the dark, clammy space, she felt her Guardian powers whooshing through her with new force. "Sam, there must be a shadow creature really close by now!" As she spoke, a banner of fog swirled up in front of

them. It formed into a column.

Sam gave a yelp, and his torch slipped from his fingers and fell to the floor, rolling a few inches away. "What's going on?" he cried. "Where did that fog come from?"

"I don't know," said Sophie, watching the white mist warily. "But I don't like it."

A shiver ran through the fog, and it suddenly became a tall, thin creature with grey skin, a large mouth and the longest, boniest fingers Sophie had ever seen.

"Whoa!" Sam said, stumbling backwards.

With a growl, the fog-thing charged straight at them!

Sophie reacted with superspeed, grabbing Sam out of the way just in time. The creature shot past, swung round in the cave entrance and faced them again.

"Leave us alone!" said Sophie fiercely, standing in front of Sam. "I'm Sophie Smith. I'm the Guardian!"

"So?" the creature snarled. "Fog Boggarts are not scared of anyone!" It lunged at them again.

Sophie spun round, her foot kicking out hard. She expected to feel the creature's body, but her foot went straight through it. It was like kicking a ghost! The creature laughed as Sophie fell to the ground.

"You cannot hurt a Fog Boggart, Guardian, but *I* can hurt you and your friend!"

He lashed out at Sophie with his long bony fingers. She ducked to the ground, feeling the damp soil and leaves beneath her hands.

"Leave her alone!" Sam was scrabbling about on the dark floor, looking for something to use as a weapon.

Sophie rolled swiftly to one side, her heart pounding. How could she fight something like this? Before she could jump to her feet, the Fog Boggart was upon her. Its ghostly fingers clutched her arm, seeming to freeze her in place.

As she watched in horror, its mouth drew closer, opening wider and wider...

3

Escape!

idn't you hear me? I said leave her alone!" yelled Sam. Finally, finding a branch on the floor, he grabbed it up and started for the Fog Boggart.

The monster swung towards him with a hiss. "You keep out of this, boy!"

"No way!" As Sam strode forwards, his foot kicked the fallen torch, and light streamed through the cavern. "Get away from her!" he shouted, waving the branch threateningly.

The Fog Boggart gave a screeching cry and leapt back. "Stop! Stop it!"

Sam kept advancing. With a strangled shriek, the Fog Boggart threw its hands over its face and ran away out of the cave and into the trees.

"Yeah, and don't come back!" Sam yelled after it. Then he let out a shaky breath, dropping the branch to the floor.

"Sam, you were brilliant!" Sophie gasped as she struggled to her feet. "But – how did you scare it off?"

He shook his head, looking dazed. "I don't know!"

They stared at each other.

Sophie shivered as she remembered the feel of the creature's icy fingers. "Well, however you did it – let's get out of here before it comes back!"

Sam nodded. "Good idea!" He grabbed up his torch, and they hurried back to the waterfall and down the track that led to Sophie's garden.

Neither of them felt like doing any more exploring right then.

"Back safe and sound!" said Sophie in relief as they climbed the fence.

"That Fog Boggart thing was seriously scary," agreed Sam.

There was a rustle of leaves and Sophie's twin brother, Anthony, popped out from behind a bush. "What was seriously scary?" he demanded, as Sophie and Sam both leapt about a metre into the air.

Sophie opened and shut her mouth, not knowing what to say.

Anthony folded his arms over his chest. "Come on, what are you two losers up to? You've been sneaking round for the last few weeks and acting really odd. What were you doing in the woods?"

"Collecting mushrooms!" Sam burst out. "We've got, er... a mushroom collecting club. And some of the mushrooms we've just seen are really poisonous, terrifying actually, seriously scary. Isn't that right, Soph?"

"That's right," Sophie said quickly. "Scary mushrooms. Brr!" She pretended to shudder.

Anthony snorted. "You two are such weirdos!

And to think I thought you might have been doing something interesting!" He marched away.

Sophie raised her eyebrows at Sam. "A mushroom collecting club?"

He grinned. "I know, but at least it got rid of him."

"For now." Sophie watched as her brother disappeared into the house. "He mustn't ever know about the shadow creatures, Sam. Remember what Grandpa said – most people can't handle finding out about them."

"We'll be extra careful from now on," agreed Sam.

They headed back to the house too. "Let's find Grandpa and tell him about the Fog Boggart," whispered Sophie, glancing around to make sure Anthony wasn't nearby.

Grandpa was reading in his bedroom. As usual, he was dressed all in black. His grey hair was cut close to his head and he looked very fit. He went running and swimming every day.

"Grandpa, we need to talk to you," said Sophie. She caught sight of Anthony looking out from his bedroom further down the corridor and shut the door firmly behind them. "We went into the woods and saw a new shadow creature," she said in a low voice.

"It was really horrible!" Sam added. "It was something called a Fog Boggart."

Grandpa's forehead creased as he put his book aside. "I've never met one of those."

They quickly told him everything that had happened. "It was almost like a ghost," finished Sophie. "I couldn't kick it or hit it, it was like fighting air. Sam got rid of it in the end, but we don't know how – it just seemed to be scared, for some reason."

Grandpa frowned. "Hmm, I remember reading something in the Shadow Files about creatures made of mist, maybe they're similar. Have you got the Shadow Files with you, Sophie?"

Sophie nodded and took a fat leather book from one of her pockets. The Shadow Files was a notebook that had been kept by all the previous Guardians, with notes about the different shadow creatures they'd met. Clues also appeared by magic in the pages to help each new Guardian find the shadow gems if they needed to.

Grandpa flicked through the thin pages. "Yes, here's the creature I was thinking about." He held the book out, showing them a picture of a

little round fat creature about the size of a rabbit. Sophie and Sam stared. Apart from the fact that the thing was coloured pale grey, it was nothing like the creature they had just seen.

"*Made of mist,*" Sam read out from the notes. "*And so impossible to hurt or hold, Mist Imps are shy, but can be mischievous. Like Chameleon Gnomes, they can change their appearance, but have also been known to mist people's minds and control their thoughts.*" He squinted at the page. "Then there's a bit that has a stain over it... I can't really make it out."

"Well, it doesn't matter – that's definitely not what we saw," said Sophie. "Isn't there anything about Fog Boggarts in there?"

But though they looked all through the files they could find no references to Fog Boggarts.

"Maybe you're the first Guardian to have seen them. You'll have to write a new entry," Grandpa told Sophie.

Sophie started to answer, and then saw something in the book that made her heart skip.

"Hey, look!" She pointed to a page on Puffball Pixies. "There's a clue here! It's for the blue gem!"

"What does it say?" asked Sam, peering over her shoulder.

Sophie quickly read the clue out:

"Between the hours of nine
And three fifteen,
The blue gem's there
But can't be seen,
Behind a locked door
Where playtime dwells.
Search in a corner
Search very well."

Sophie, Sam and Grandpa all looked at each other. "But what does that mean?" wondered

Sophie. "Why can the gem only be seen between nine and three fifteen?"

Grandpa shook his head. "It doesn't make sense. The gems don't appear and disappear."

Sam looked thoughtful. "No, wait! I reckon it doesn't mean the gem vanishes – just that we usually only go to the place where it's hidden during those times!"

Sophie frowned. "But where can it be? Shops stay open until six and…"

"Sophie!" Sam widened his eyes as he urged her to get it. "Come on, where do we go every day, Monday to Friday, between nine and three fifteen?"

Suddenly the penny dropped. "School!" Sophie gasped.

"Of course!" said Grandpa, clapping Sam on the back. "Well done!"

Sam glowed. Sophie felt warm inside too. When she had first become Guardian, Grandpa had been very unhappy that Sam knew about the Shadow Realm, but gradually, it seemed he was beginning to realise how useful her best friend could be.

"This is great!" she exclaimed happily. "If the gem's at school, we can look for it tomorrow. What do you think the rest of the clue means, about 'where playtime dwells'?"

"Maybe it's hidden in the PE store?" suggested Sam, scratching his head.

"Yes! I bet that's it!" exclaimed Sophie. "Good one, Sam."

"Well, if it's not, you'll just have to check every locked place in the whole school," said Grandpa grimly. "We *must* find that gem!"

Sophie nodded. Enthusiasm was rushing

through her, banishing thoughts of the Fog Boggart in the woods. They had the clue for the next gem. She couldn't wait to start trying to find it!

In her excitement, she didn't notice the swirl of mist outside the window. The Fog Boggarts had heard everything they had said…

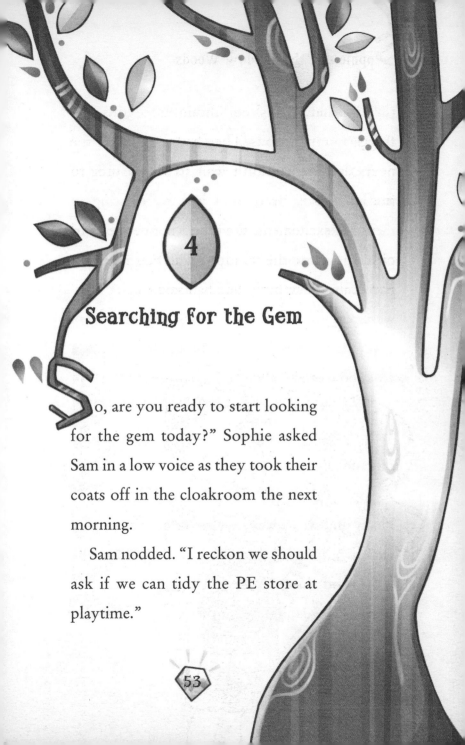

4

Searching for the Gem

"So, are you ready to start looking for the gem today?" Sophie asked Sam in a low voice as they took their coats off in the cloakroom the next morning.

Sam nodded. "I reckon we should ask if we can tidy the PE store at playtime."

"Good idea," agreed Sophie. "It's got to be there!"

As they went into their classroom, Anthony and his friends, Brett and Chris, were sitting on their desks talking. Behind them were a group of girls, Ria, Tara and Daisy, who all had matching ponytails and sparkly slides in their hair. They were playing with their Fluffies, toys that were covered in pastel-coloured fur and looked like a cross between an alien and a baby.

"*Wanna cuddle?*" said one of the Fluffies, making a whirring sound as it blinked its ridiculously cute blue eyes.

Sophie grimaced. Mrs B had bought her a Fluffy and was always trying to get her to play with it, but Sophie thought they were gross. The only good thing about Fluffies was that they were so disgustingly cute that she and Sam had

used them to fight off the Swamp Boggles the week before!

Sam leaned against his desk, frowning around them. "I never noticed how many locked cupboards are in the school before," he whispered. "If it's not in the PE store, then where do you think—"

"Boredom alert!" called Anthony across the room. "Sam's talking! "

Sophie glared at her brother. "Leave Sam alone!" she snapped.

Anthony's pale blue eyes gleamed. "Standing up for your boyfriend, are you? I saw you two yesterday, going into the woods together, holding hands."

Brett and Chris sniggered.

"We were *not* holding hands!" Sophie said quickly, as she saw the rest of the class suddenly take notice.

"You were in there ages," Anthony went on.
"I bet you were…" he paused and grinned round
at the class, "… *kissing.*"

Brett and Chris hooted with laughter.

"So are you and Sophie going out, Sam?" Ria
called.

"No!" Sam exclaimed hotly. "Of course we're
not!"

"Is she your *girlfriend*?" cooed Tara, waggling
her Fluffy at them.

"NO!" said both Sam and Sophie together.

Just then, Mrs Wilson, their teacher, came in. "Come on, everyone," she said, clapping her hands. "You should be reading your books before school. You know the rules."

The giggling and teasing stopped and everyone sat down. Sophie's cheeks were on fire. Anthony could be *so* annoying. She wished a shadow creature would come and get him! She didn't dare look at Sam. She knew he must be as embarrassed as she was. Thankfully, Mrs Wilson was strict, and the class soon settled down.

Then, later that morning, during their science lesson, she led them all up to the roof, where a wind turbine had been set up as an experiment. Sophie stood and stared with the others. There wasn't much to see – just big windmill blades spinning round in the breeze, and a couple of wires leading to a large brick-shaped battery.

Sam was fascinated, of course! "It works like my wind-up torch, I think," he murmured to Sophie. "The wind turns the blades, which make energy go into the battery. Then the battery can be used to power things." He frowned. "Though I wonder what would happen if…" He put up his hand. "Mrs Wilson, what would happen if there was no wind so the blades weren't turning round, but you connected the battery anyway?"

Anthony sighed loudly. "Geek-brain," he whispered.

"Enough," Mrs Wilson said sternly. She turned to Sam. "It's an interesting thought, Sam. If I left the battery connected and there wasn't any wind, we'd probably find the blades would start to spin back in the other direction. They'd be powered by the battery."

"Cool," said Sam, his eyes shining.

Sophie heard the snorts from Anthony's group and sighed inwardly. Sometimes Sam made it very easy for them to pick on him!

At break time, she and Sam asked if they could tidy the PE store. Sophie's heart thumped excitedly as they cleared it out, but there was no sign of the gem on any of the crowded corner shelves.

Sinking back on to her heels, Sophie let out a disappointed breath. She had been so sure that this was what the clue meant by 'playtime'! "I really thought it was going to be here."

"I know," said Sam. He made a face and started putting things back in the cupboard. "Well, we'll just have to think of something else, I guess."

After break, the wind dropped, and at lunchtime a thick fog suddenly fell over the school. Looking out of the window, Sophie felt a strange unease come over her. It seemed a bit of a coincidence that there should be a fog when the day before she and Sam had seen shadow creatures called *Fog* Boggarts. Could the Fog Boggarts be the cause of it somehow?

"It's indoor play," Sam reminded her. "Do you want to see if we can clear out the art store too? Art's sort of like 'playtime'."

I'm being silly, decided Sophie. Just because there were Fog Boggarts about didn't mean that every fog she saw was suspicious. Besides, if they *were* behind this then she'd feel the magic tingling through her.

"Good idea," she told Sam.

But just as they reached the staffroom, they

saw Mrs Wilson come out, bundled up in a coat and looking pale. She was with Mr Bryan, their tall, cheerful head teacher. "I don't know what's the matter with me," she was saying. "About fifteen minutes ago, I just started to feel really sick."

"Well, get yourself home and hopefully you'll feel better by tomorrow," Mr Bryan comforted her.

"But I haven't organised any work for my class, or—"

"Don't worry," Mr Bryan reassured her. "We'll cope."

Before Mrs Wilson could answer, all the lights suddenly went out! Sophie started, looking around in surprise.

"Oh, dear," said Mr Bryan, running a hand through his hair. "A fuse must have blown. I'd better check it out."

"Poor Mrs Wilson," said Sophie to Sam as their teacher left, and Mr Bryan started checking the fuse box by the front door. "She seemed OK this morning. I wonder what's the matter with her?"

Just then, a young woman appeared in the school entrance porch and tapped on the glass.

Mr Bryan went to the door. "Hello. Can I help you?"

"Oh, hello." The woman smiled. She was very pretty, with shoulder-length blonde hair and wide-spaced, large grey eyes. "My name is Miss Waters. I'm a teacher, and I was wondering how to go about being put on your list of supply staff. I've got all the paperwork you need right here." She patted her bag.

"Well, we'd have to check your references of course and... and..." Mr Bryan's brisk voice trailed off. For a moment he just stared at the

teacher in front of him and then a dreamy
expression crossed his face.

"You don't happen to need a supply teacher
today by any chance, do you?" Miss Waters asked.

"Well, actually, yes," Mr Bryan answered,
sounding dazed. "One of our teachers has just
gone home sick."

Miss Waters beamed. "Why don't I cover for her?"

"Oh, do, please!" Mr Bryan held the school door open. "Come in. I'm sorry about the lighting in here. The electricity seems to be working OK, so I don't know why the lights aren't. It would happen on a day like this too," he said, motioning to the fog outside the windows. "It's going to be a dark afternoon in school until the electrician comes out!"

"That's all right, I don't mind the dark at all." Miss Waters dimpled at him as she stepped inside.

Sophie felt a prickle race across her scalp. "Isn't that a bit weird?" she hissed to Sam. "Mrs Wilson goes home, and a new supply teacher just turns up, completely by chance?"

Sam nodded. "Yeah, and Mr Bryan asks her to teach us, just like that? Without checking

anything about her?"

Sophie had noticed something else too. "And how did she know that it was a female teacher she was replacing? She said, 'I could certainly cover for *her.*'"

"I suppose she could have seen Mrs Wilson leaving," Sam suggested.

But Sophie couldn't squash the worried feeling. "I don't like this," she muttered. "I think something sinister's going on."

"You mean something to do with the shadow creatures?" said Sam uneasily.

Sophie glanced at the fog outside. It looked thicker than ever. "Maybe," she said. But in that case, why wasn't she feeling the tingle of her Guardian magic?

"Now come in here, my dear," Mr Bryan was saying to the supply teacher as he led her towards the staffroom. "I'm sure you'd like a cup of tea."

Miss Waters smiled up at him. "That's very kind of you, Mr Bryan – or can I call you by your first name?"

Mr Bryan blushed like a tomato. "Oh yes, of course, it's… er… it's Dan."

Miss Waters put her hand on his arm. "A cup of tea would be just lovely, *Dan.*"

As Mr Bryan went even redder and opened the staffroom door, the new supply teacher saw Sophie and Sam. She smiled straight at them, and Sophie stiffened. Miss Waters's mouth seemed very wide somehow. "Hello, children," she said.

"Hi," muttered Sophie, staring at the supply teacher's red lips. What was going on? Now her mouth looked totally normal!

Miss Waters continued on into the staffroom

with Mr Bryan. Sophie blinked as the door shut behind them. Had she only imagined it? "OK, I've got a *very* bad feeling," she said slowly.

"I've got a very good feeling," sighed Sam. "Isn't Miss Waters lovely?"

"*What?*" Sophie spun round, staring at him.

Sam was gazing at the staffroom door. "She's *so* beautiful, and I bet she's really clever too. I'm really glad she's going to be teaching us." Smiling soppily, he drifted back towards into their classroom.

Sophie gaped. What had happened? A moment ago, Sam had been normal, and now he was acting as oddly as Mr Bryan. She heard the supply teacher's laugh trilling out from the staffroom and felt a shiver run down her spine.

Something strange was going on. But what?

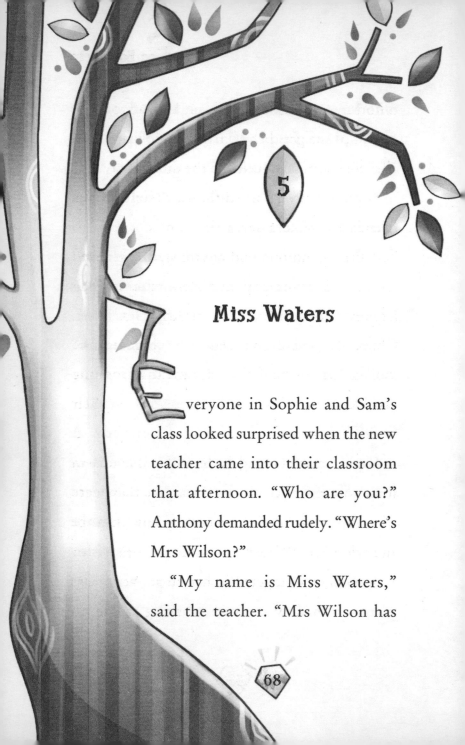

5

Miss Waters

Everyone in Sophie and Sam's class looked surprised when the new teacher came into their classroom that afternoon. "Who are you?" Anthony demanded rudely. "Where's Mrs Wilson?"

"My name is Miss Waters," said the teacher. "Mrs Wilson has

unfortunately been taken ill, so I'm here to teach you until she gets better. Isn't that lovely for us all?" She beamed at them in the dull light.

Sophie waited for Anthony or one of his friends to make a sarcastic comment, but to her surprise no one said anything. She glanced around. Everyone in her class was smiling happily back at Miss Waters! Anthony, Brett, Chris, Ria, Tara and Daisy... wherever she looked, she saw her fellow classmates all looking just like Sam, with dazed expressions on their faces.

Sophie was starting to feel like she was in some sort of freaky movie. It was like they were all under a spell! Remembering how strange and wide Miss Waters's mouth had looked for a moment, she fidgeted in her chair. Was Miss Waters a shadow creature working magic on everyone, somehow? But how *could* she be? Sophie would have felt her Guardian powers kicking in. And she hadn't.

Miss Waters's grey eyes fell on her. "Are you all right, dear?"

Sophie froze. "Yes," she replied warily.

"What's your name?"

"Sophie Smith."

The teacher stared at her, her grey eyes as cold as two pools of ice. "So, *you're* Sophie Smith. Well, Sophie, I like pupils to sit quietly in my classes. If you can't sit still on your chair I'm afraid you'll have to come and stand out here at the front." She pointed to the bin. "Over there. By the bin. You'll have to stand with the rubbish until you learn how to behave."

Sophie went to the front of the class, her cheeks burning red. Anthony and his friends

sniggered. Instead of telling them off, the supply teacher smiled. "I imagine Sophie can be a bit annoying," she commented archly to the class.

"You're telling me, Miss!" said Anthony. "I have to live with her!"

Stung, Sophie glanced at Sam for support, but her best friend was gazing adoringly at the teacher just like everyone else.

"Well, she'll soon learn that I won't stand for annoying pupils in *my* class!" Miss Waters laughed.

Anthony and his friends chortled. Sophie glared at her feet.

"Now, I've had a look at your timetable and I know you usually do numeracy now," Miss Waters went on. "But I think we should do something more fun. We're going to have a whole afternoon of doing art!" She smiled. For an uneasy second Sophie thought she saw that too-wide look to her mouth again... then it was gone.

"Let's get started!" Miss Waters said, and everyone cheered.

It was the worst afternoon at school of Sophie's life. When Miss Waters finally let Sophie sit back down and do some drawing, she laughed at Sophie's picture of a dog, saying it looked more like an elephant, holding it up for everyone in the class to laugh at too. Then she made Sophie wash out all the old paint and glue pots while everyone else was making models.

"Here we are, another one!" Anthony said, sloshing a pot full of glue into the sink where Sophie was washing up. The water splashed all over her top and trousers. "Whoops!" Anthony grinned.

Miss Waters was passing. "Sophie, you should be more careful! Now, children. I just have to get something. I know I can trust you to stay quietly in here and be good."

"Yes, Miss Waters!" everyone chorused except Sophie, who scowled.

"Excellent. See you in a few minutes." The teacher slipped through the door that led to the hall.

Sophie dashed across the room to Sam. "Sam! Quick!" she hissed. "We have to follow her!"

Sam blinked, looking up dreamily from his model. "But she told us to stay here."

Sophie could have shaken him. "*So*?"

"So we have to do what we're told. She's so wonderful," smiled Sam.

"Perfect!" said Jake from beside him.

"And pretty!" sighed Nasim.

Sophie stamped her foot in frustration. She wasn't going to get any sense out of any of them! There was only one thing for it – leaving them all to their models, she slipped out into the hall.

Miss Waters was walking slowly down the corridor. There was something hidden in her hand that she kept glancing at. As she walked past the PE cupboard, she checked whatever it was. Then she walked past the door that led to Mr Bryan's classroom.

"Nothing," she muttered. She stopped a bit further by the door that led into the art room. "Aha," she breathed. "This looks more like it!"

Pressed against the wall, Sophie stared. What was the teacher looking for, and what was she holding? Something definitely wasn't right – and she had to find out what it was!

As Miss Waters headed towards the door that led into the art room, Sophie stepped out of the shadows. "What are you doing?" she demanded.

Miss Waters swung round and for a moment her pretty face was transformed. Her eyes bulged and her mouth opened wide as she hissed, her hands rising in the air like claws. Sophie's blood went cold as she stared in shock.

With a snarl, Miss Waters started towards her, but just then there was the sound of a door opening. "Well, hello, hello, what's happening here?" Mr Bryan's cheery voice rang out from behind them.

Miss Waters's face instantly changed back to its usual sweet expression. "Oh, hello, Mr Bryan, she said as the head teacher walked over through the gloomy light. "I was just about to pop into the art room to ask if they had any glue spreaders we could borrow, and Sophie came to tell me we needed some more glue too. We are having a rather creative afternoon," she told the head teacher. "It's so important for children to express themselves, don't you think?"

"Oh, absolutely," said Mr Bryan, staring at her as if he couldn't take his eyes off her. "Whatever you want to do, Miss Waters, I am completely happy with. And may I say what a delight it is to have you in the school." He picked up her hand and lightly kissed it!

Miss Waters giggled coyly. "Will you want me back tomorrow then?"

"Oh, definitely. I'll ring Mrs Wilson and tell her not to worry about coming back until she's completely better."

"Wonderful!" exclaimed Miss Waters. She gave Sophie a fake smile. "Now run along back to class, darling child." She turned back to Mr Bryan. "I'll just nip into the art room."

"Nothing would give me greater pleasure than to come with you," he declared.

Sophie saw a look of annoyance flash across Miss Waters's face, and then the supply teacher smiled. "That would be lovely, *Dan.*" They walked off together arm in arm. Sophie rushed

back to her classroom.

"Sam!" she exclaimed, flinging herself in the seat beside him. "I just saw Miss Waters looking round the hall for something, and then she hissed at me!"

Sam gaped at her in disbelief. "*Hissed* at you!"

"Yes! Oh, Sam, I'm sure she's something to do with the shadow creatures, and I think she's looking for the gem!"

Sam was already shaking his head. "No, she's just a supply teacher and she's great, Sophie."

"She is *not* great!" Sophie exclaimed in frustration. "She's been really mean to me, you know she has."

Sam hesitated. For a moment, Sophie thought he was about to agree with her and her heart leapt, but just then the door opened and Miss Waters came back in. "Hello, everyone," she trilled.

Sam's face instantly relaxed, and he beamed back.

Miss Waters's eyes fell on Sophie and her tone changed. "Sophie! Get back to the washing up!"

Sophie hesitated, but what could she do? Everyone in the school seemed to be under the supply teacher's spell apart from her. She stomped over to the sink. If Sam wouldn't believe

her that Miss Waters was up to something then no one would. *Grandpa!* she thought suddenly. Of course! She'd be able to talk to him when she got home!

She glanced round over her shoulder. The teacher was staring straight at her, her grey eyes glinting. Sophie lifted her chin and met her gaze with a scowl. No matter what anyone else thought, if Miss Waters was trying to find the gem then Sophie was going to stop her!

6

What is Going On?

o, just because your supply teacher wasn't very nice to you, you think she's something to do with the shadow creatures?" Grandpa looked at Sophie, his grey eyebrows raised.

She paced up and down his room. "Grandpa, she hissed and snarled at me!"

"You said she got cross because you were out of the classroom without permission." Grandpa folded his arms. "That doesn't sound like strange behaviour to me."

"No, it was the way she looked and sounded," said Sophie. "She seems to have cast a spell on everyone. Even *Anthony* likes her. That's weird!"

Her grandfather hesitated and then nodded. "OK, I admit that *is* strange. I'll come to school with you tomorrow and see what I make of her. I suppose she might be a shadow creature in disguise."

"But then I'd feel the Guardian magic when I was around her," Sophie pointed out. Even so, she felt a weight drop off her shoulders. It was such a relief to know that she wasn't alone any more! "Thanks, Grandpa," she said. "I guess we'll see tomorrow."

As Sophie went to the door she stopped, her fingers on the handle. She was feeling very mixed up inside. Slowly, she turned back to Grandpa. "It's horrible – having something going on at school," she admitted. "I mean, I'm getting used to shadow creatures in the woods and other places, but... school's where I go to be normal."

Her grandfather had never been the understanding, cuddly type of grandparent, but to Sophie's surprise he gave her a sympathetic look. "I know, child. Once you're the Guardian, even the normal bits of life are never quite the same again."

"Oh," Sophie said in a small voice.

Coming over to her, Grandpa squeezed her shoulder. "You're doing a good job, you know," he told her. "A *very* good job."

Sophie felt a bit better. She managed a smile.

84

"I'll be doing an even better job when I find the blue gem."

"Tomorrow," Grandpa repeated.

In the morning, Grandpa and Sophie stopped at Sam's house to collect him. Sophie and Sam lived on the same road, and always walked to school together. But this morning, Sam's mum shook her head. "I'm sorry, but Sam's already gone into school," she told them. "He wanted to see if he could help this new teacher with anything. He seems very keen on her."

"Everyone is," sighed Sophie.

She and Grandpa carried on by themselves. As they got closer to school, Sophie's eyes widened. It was completely surrounded by fog! It swirled around them in dense patches, making it hard to see. The lights were still off in the

school too, so that it looked very dim in the
classrooms as they came up the drive.

"See, Grandpa?" whispered Sophie. "Something
weird's going on!"

He frowned, gazing around them at the fog. "Maybe," he admitted. "Let's meet this new teacher of yours then."

Leading the way into the classroom, Sophie saw Miss Waters sitting by her desk, surrounded by pupils. Many of them had brought her presents. There were bunches of flowers, boxes of chocolates, perfume, bubble bath and home-made cards. Sam was holding a picture he had drawn. Even Anthony was there, with a few wilting flowers he had clearly picked from someone's garden along the way.

"This just isn't right," Sophie muttered to Grandpa. "Look at them all! Something *has* to be going on; no one is ever like this with a supply teacher!"

"Hmm," said Grandpa, watching with narrowed eyes.

Just then Miss Waters looked up and saw them. "Good morning!" She beamed at Grandpa full on.

The change happened so quickly that Sophie didn't even see it coming. "Good morning," Grandpa sighed, smiling back at the teacher. Sophie heard the dreamy note in his voice and her heart sank like a stone.

"Grandpa!" she whispered, pulling urgently

at his arm. Not him as well!

"What is it, Sophie?" he said when they were away from the teacher. "And why on earth were you so worried about Miss Waters? She seems perfectly lovely!"

Sophie gaped at him in dismay. "But—"

"Be good today, Sophie," Grandpa told her, drifting off out of the classroom. "Don't upset Miss Waters, now."

Sophie stared around her. She didn't know what to do. Now no one at all believed her! She watched the other pupils all competing to talk to Miss Waters. Not even the sight of Mr Bryan coming in with a poem he had written for the supply teacher could cheer Sophie up.

Mr Bryan took Miss Waters's hand and declared: *"Roses are red, violets are blue, you are so sweet, I…"* The head teacher drew a picture of

a heart in the air, *"... heart you!"*

Sophie wanted to throw up. Gross! Mr Bryan stared goofily at Miss Waters.

"What a darling poem!" Miss Waters said. "I'm so glad you've come in to see me, Dan. I think it would be a simply wonderful idea if the whole school, all the children and all the teachers, took part in a day of drama!"

"Excellent!" declared Mr Bryan.

"I will organise it," Miss Waters told him, her grey eyes glinting. "We'll rehearse in the hall all morning. I want everyone..." her gaze swept over Sophie, "... *everyone* to be there."

Straight after the registers had been taken, the entire school trooped into the hall. Sophie trailed along at the back of her class. Why did Miss Waters want them all in the hall for the entire morning? Maybe she wanted to search the school, but how could she if she was going to be teaching the whole time?

As she sat down beside Sam at the back of the hall, Sophie overheard Mr Bryan talking to Miss Waters. "I'm sorry that the lights aren't working yet. The electrician came last night but he's stumped. There doesn't seem to be anything wrong and yet the lights just aren't working. He's coming back this afternoon. I've got the stage lights out for you from the drama cupboard. I'll bring them into the hall now if you like."

"Oh, no," Miss Waters said swiftly. "We'll be fine like this. It's lovely of you to suggest it, but don't worry at all. Now do come and sit down." She guided him into a chair at the side of the hall and then made her way to the front and clapped

her hands. "Right everyone, let's begin!"

As Miss Waters started to tell the school the story they were going to be acting out that morning, Sophie got out the Shadow Files from her bag. Hiding them on her lap, she began to flick through the pages. *Please let there be something in here that will help me,* she thought. Were there shadow creatures that could change their appearance so thoroughly that even Guardian magic didn't work?

Change their appearance.

Sophie frowned. The words rang a bell somehow. She thought back. Yes, it had been the day she had been looking in the Shadow Files with Grandpa and Sam...

She turned quickly to the page in the Shadow Files they'd been looking at in Grandpa's bedroom the day she and Sam had seen the Fog Boggart.

Of course! *Mist Imps!* A drawing of a round, small shadow creature looked out at Sophie. Her eyes skipped over the notes: *Made of mist and so impossible to hurt or hold, Mist Imps are known for their love of mischief. Like Chameleon Gnomes, they can change their appearance, but have also been known to mist people's minds and control their thoughts.*

Sophie caught her breath. So there *were* some shadow creatures who could control people's minds! She stared at the stained part of the page, searching for more clues. Squinting, she could just make out three tiny letters at the bottom: *P.T.O.*

Sophie knew that meant: *Please Turn Over.*

She quickly turned the page, her heart beating fast. On the back was an extra scribble: *Also worth noting: although Mist Imps are unable to mist the Guardian's mind they can cloak themselves with magic so the Guardian's powers will not detect them."*

Sophie gave a strangled squeak. So Miss Waters could be a shadow creature after all! She could be cloaking herself so Sophie's powers didn't kick in. *I bet she is, I just bet she is,* thought Sophie. It all made sense now. But why had the teacher got them all into the hall? What was she planning?

Sophie pulled Sam's arm. "Sam!" she whispered.

"Sssh! I'm listening!"

She thrust the book at him. "This is important. Miss Waters really *is* a shadow creature! Read this!"

Sam read the notes and followed Sophie's finger as she pointed out the tiny words over the page. A look of confusion flickered across his face, and then he shook his head stubbornly. "She's not a shadow creature."

"She is! She's using mind control and stopping me from sensing her," Sophie said. "Sam, listen to me!" Gripping his hand, she looked desperately into his eyes.

She heard Anthony snicker a bit further along

the row. He whispered in a sing-song voice: *"Sophie and Sam, up a tree..."*

Sophie ignored him; she was too busy staring at Sam, willing him to believe her. For a moment she thought he was going to turn away, but then he hesitated and rubbed his head. "I feel so weird... Miss Waters..." he glanced at the teacher, "... is she really a shadow creature?"

She nodded hard. "Yes! Please, Sam, you've got to trust me!"

"I do," said Sam. "You're my best friend." Then he blinked, as if he'd just heard what he'd said. Something seemed to change in his eyes – and all at once he was Sam again. "Sophie!" he hissed, grabbing her arm. "Miss Waters *is* controlling everyone – what are we going to do?"

Yes! Sophie felt like punching the air. Finally,

Sam believed her and sounded normal again! "I don't know, but I'm sure Miss Waters is looking for the gem. Yesterday, I saw her…" Sophie broke off with a gasp. "My Guardian powers!" A familiar tingling sensation was rushing through her. "I can feel them!"

"But I thought Miss Waters was cloaking herself from you?" Sam said.

A horrible thought hit Sophie. "Maybe there are other shadow creatures in the school who *aren't* cloaking themselves."

Sam swallowed. "And she's keeping us all in here so that no one gets in their way. Sounds like we'd better go and have a look around."

Sophie nodded. Taking care not to be seen, they dropped to their hands and knees and edged their way to the door. Mr Bryan was sitting beside it.

"We're just going to the toilet," Sophie said to him as they ducked past. The head teacher nodded. He seemed much too interested in gazing adoringly at Miss Waters to worry about them.

Sophie and Sam emerged into the corridor between their classroom and the art room. With everyone in the hall, the school felt eerily quiet. The open drama cupboard was at the end of the corridor, the stage lights on their stands half in and half out of the store.

"Isn't it dark?" said Sam, glancing around them. "It's really weird, the way the lights went out just when Miss Waters arrived. I bet it has something to do with her."

Suddenly it all came together. "Sam, that's it!" gasped Sophie, clutching his arm. "The Fog Boggarts must hate bright light! It was your *torch* that scared the one in the woods off – and that's why Miss Waters has done something to the lights in the school!"

Sam's mouth fell open. He hit himself on the forehead. "Of course! Light burns away fog –

why didn't I think of that?"

Sophie was just about to reply when she glanced through the window into the classroom. "Look!" she exclaimed in horror. The room was full of swirling fog!

7

Fog Boggart Attack!

As Sophie and Sam watched, the white mist changed into nine tall, thin Fog Boggarts. All had long fingers, grey skin, large mouths and deep, dark eyes. But it was the one in the middle of the room who drew Sophie's gaze – the one who was holding a glowing iron

key in his bony hands!

"It's the Fog Boggarts!" Sophie whispered frantically, pulling Sam down under the window.

"Loads of them. What are we going to do?" demanded Sam.

The Guardian powers pounded through Sophie like a drumbeat. What had she been scared of? She wanted to leap, fight, attack! She jumped to her feet. "Come on, let's get rid of them!"

Sam yanked her back down. "Wait, Soph! You can't just march in there. Your kicks can't hurt them, remember? We need to think of a plan!"

Reluctantly, Sophie stayed where she was. Pressing against the wall, she could hear the Fog Boggarts's voices through the bricks.

"It must be here somewhere! Queen Spindle Fingers told us the key glowed when she came into this room yesterday."

"Our queen looks good as a human, doesn't she?" she heard another say.

"Almost good enough to swallow!" said the first voice.

"Hur! Hur! Hur!" The sound of laughter echoed from the room.

"Let's find this gem, Bone Cruncher. Hold the key up."

There was a pause and then the voices got louder. "It's glowing brightest over here, near this wall."

Sophie frowned. "They think the gem's in the art room because the key's

glowing, but how can it be? The clue said it's behind a locked door."

Sam looked at the open drama cupboard beside them. "*That's* usually locked!" he pointed out. "The gem could be hidden inside, and that's why the key's glowing when it's near this wall."

Sophie's pulse leapt as she suddenly realised: *In a place where playtime dwells...* "Sam!" she cried. "*Playtime!* Drama is all about putting on plays!"

Without waiting for an answer, she lunged for the drama cupboard and started pulling things out. A dusty crown... a telephone... a plastic skull...

Search in a corner, she thought, remembering the clue. Pushing aside a cardboard box full of clothes for dressing up, she scooted all the way into the cupboard and ran her hand along

the dusty shelf. At first
there was nothing, and
her spirits sank. Then
she felt something small
and round and closed
her fingers around it.
A blue gem sparkled
in her hand!

"I've got it!" she
whispered, holding it
up in triumph.

Sam's face lit up. "Now all we need to do is
get rid of the Fog Boggarts!"

Sophie nodded worriedly as she tucked the
gem safely into her pocket. "If only we had your
torch – lots of torches, in fact!"

Sam grinned suddenly. "We might not have
torches, but we've got something even better!"

He pointed at the two stage lights.

"Brilliant! Come on!" Sophie said.

They crawled over. The stage lights were massive, and were on metal stands with wheels. Silently, they pushed the lights towards the art room door.

Sam plugged the lights into the socket in the corridor wall. "OK, I'll turn the socket on and at the same moment you push both lights through the door. Let's see how the Fog Boggarts like this!"

Sophie could hear the boggarts moving about in the classroom, still searching for the gem. Thank goodness everyone else was in the hall! "Are you ready?" she breathed. Sam nodded.

"One... two... THREE!" Sophie gave the stands a push and the bulbs burst into blinding light. "Take that!" she cried.

"ARGH!" The Fog Boggarts staggered backwards as the light burst through the gloom in the art room. All nine of them retreated into the shadows, shrieking and covering their faces.

"It's working!" exclaimed Sophie.

"But not well enough," said Sam, chewing his

lip. "It's holding the boggarts back, but they're not going away!"

Sophie realised he was right. The boggarts were gathering together, pointing at the lights and whispering. Suddenly they started picking things up and throwing them at the lights!

"They're trying to break the bulbs!" realised Sophie. Her Guardian powers tingled through her. She leapt high in the air, twisting in a tae kwon do move as she kicked things away from the lights. Books, a toy tractor, a measuring jug and a ruler. Items from the art room went flying all around them as she spun, feet flashing.

Sam was lunging and diving too, trying his best to bat things away from the lights. "We need another plan!" he gasped.

"Yes, well spotted!" cried Sophie, bounding upwards again as a globe of the world hurtled through the air. She half-turned with a flying kick, sending it bouncing off the wall.

The Fog Boggarts edged forwards, keeping to the shadows but throwing more and more things: a plastic dinosaur followed a set of scales. With a pair of spinning leaps Sophie kicked the items away and then raced for the lamps, shoving them towards the boggarts again. The creatures shrieked and shrank back, shielding their eyes.

"I've got it!" burst out Sam. Sophie rushed to his side. "The Fog Boggarts hate bright light – well, what light is brighter than sunshine?" he hissed. "There's been a fog here ever since Miss

Waters arrived, and I bet that's why. It's protecting them! So why don't we try to move the fog and let the sun shine down?"

"Just one problem!" Sophie leapt in the air again, whirling to kick aside a wooden train. It crashed against the whiteboard. "*How* exactly are we supposed to do that?"

"The wind turbine!" said Sam in a low voice. "You'll have to do it, because you can move extra fast with your Guardian superpowers. Go up on to the roof using the fire escape. Then connect the turbine to the battery. Hopefully the blades will start to turn and that will blow away the fog!"

Sophie glanced at the Fog Boggarts. They had edged nearer once more, so close now that she could see their long, spiny teeth. "But what about the boggarts?" she gasped.

Sam took a breath. "Guess you're going to have

to leave them to me!" He jumped behind the lights and twisted them round again, aiming them right at the creatures. "Take that, you foggy freaks!" he yelled. They reeled backwards with snarls and hisses. "Go, Sophie! Go!" he urged.

Sophie charged out of the classroom and out of the door into the grey, misty playground. Vaulting lightly over the gate, she leapt up the metal steps of the fire escape. In seconds she was standing on the school roof. The world seemed utterly silent. There wasn't a breath of wind, and the blades of the wind turbine were completely still.

Sophie saw the wire hanging down from the wind turbine, and remembered what Sam had told her to do. She quickly connected the wire to the battery and looked pleadingly at the motionless blades. *Work, please work*, she prayed.

For a moment nothing happened... and then

slowly the blades began to turn. Faster and faster they went until they were whooshing round, creating a fierce wind that blew Sophie's fringe back from her face and made her trousers and sweatshirt flap. "Yes!" she cried.

The wind started to move the fog away, first from the roof and then from the school. As the mist vanished, Sophie saw a patch of blue sky, and then suddenly the sun's rays slanted through, bright and warm. The plan was working! But how was Sam coping with the Fog Boggarts in the classroom?

Pounding back down the fire escape, Sophie sprinted to the art room. Bursting in through the door, she saw that one of the lights had had its bulb broken. Sam was backed up against the whiteboard, shielding himself with the remaining light while the boggarts threw things at it.

"Well?" he gasped when he saw her.

"I've done it!" she said. "The fog's…"

She broke off as the door opened and Anthony came in.

"What are you two up to? What… WAH!" He broke off with a yelp as he saw the Fog Boggarts throwing things. "MONSTERS!" he yelled. A whiteboard rubber hit Anthony square on the head. He yelped and dropped to the floor.

"Anthony!" gasped Sophie.

Chuckling evilly, two Fog Boggarts edged through the shadows towards him.

"Leave him alone!" cried Sophie. She might not like her brother, but she wasn't going to let the Fog Boggarts get their hands on him. She leapt across the room, but at that moment a new figure stepped into the open doorway.

It was Miss Waters! A shiver ran through the teacher and she transformed into a Fog Boggart herself. Her body stretched and her mouth widened.

"Queen Spindle Fingers!" The delighted cry went up from the other Fog Boggarts.

"Get them!" Miss Waters, also known as Spindle Fingers, snarled, pointing at Sophie and Sam.

Sophie's heart thudded. Oh, where was the sunshine? There was no sign of it through the windows yet. She had to do something! She pulled the blue gem out of her pocket and held it up. It sparkled in the dim light. "Here! Do you want this? Is this what you're all after?"

The Fog Boggarts reacted instantly.

"The gem!"

"Get it off her!"

"Stop her!"

"Come and get it!" Sophie sang. She raced

outside with Sam following after, her breath short in her throat. *Please, let it be sunny out here,* she thought. As the Fog Boggarts burst out of the classroom and into the playground, the last of the fog blew away. Bright sunlight shone on the Fog Boggarts. They shrieked, writhing as their bodies began to dissolve in the light.

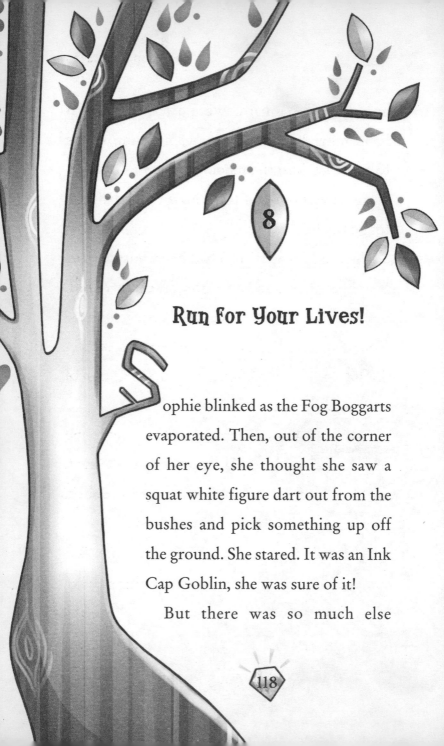

8

Run for Your Lives!

ophie blinked as the Fog Boggarts
evaporated. Then, out of the corner
of her eye, she thought she saw a
squat white figure dart out from the
bushes and pick something up off
the ground. She stared. It was an Ink
Cap Goblin, she was sure of it!

But there was so much else

going on, it was hard to see exactly what was happening. All the boggarts were yelling, trying to run back into the school, but it was too late. The sun was burning them away, melting their foggy bodies.

The Fog Boggart who had been Miss Waters hissed in fury and ran at Sophie, her mouth opening wider and wider. "You tricked us! You... you..." But even as she reached out for Sophie with her long bony fingers, the Queen of the Fog Boggarts melted away!

Suddenly all was silent, apart from the sound of the wind turbine's blades turning on the roof.

"We... we did it!" Sam stammered in shock, looking round the empty playground.

"And we got the gem!" cried Sophie. She jumped into the air, spinning and doing a flying kick.

"What about the key?" Sam exclaimed. He started to hunt around on the ground.

Sophie's spirits leapt. If they could just find the key, this would be the most amazing day ever! In a frenzy, she helped Sam look, but the key was nowhere to be found. Suddenly Sophie remembered the figure she'd seen, and groaned aloud. "Sam! I'm sure I saw an Ink Cap Goblin run out of the bushes over there. I bet it was spying, and picked up the key."

The two of them stared at each other in despair. This might have been their only chance to get the key back again and now it was gone.

Finally Sophie sighed. "Well, at least we've got the gem." She slipped it into the purse belt she wore around her waist. "Come on, we'd better go back inside. This is the longest trip to the toilet ever!"

As they shut the door behind them they heard a faint groaning noise. Anthony was standing up, swaying slightly and rubbing his head. "Where have the monsters gone?" he blurted out when he saw them.

Sophie raised her eyebrows. "Monsters? What are you talking about, Anthony?"

"There's definitely no monsters here," said Sam with a shrug.

"But I saw them! We've got to warn everyone – quick!" Anthony ran back to the hall.

Sophie and Sam chased after him. "Anthony! Stop!" yelped Sophie.

But Anthony wouldn't listen. "MONSTERS!" he screamed, bursting into the hall. "There are monsters in the school! Run! Run for your lives!"

Everyone was working in small groups with different teachers. They all stopped and stared at him.

"It's real!" Anthony cried, waving his arms about and jumping up and down. "There are monsters. Great tall grey ones with big mouths!"

Mr Bryan strode over. "Anthony, whatever are you doing? Be quiet and go back to your group, please."

"But Mr Bryan, there are monsters out there,"

panted Anthony. He pointed towards the door. "They attacked me!"

People started to giggle. Mr Bryan's frown deepened.

Sophie stepped forwards. "Um, Mr Bryan, Anthony got hit on the head," she said quickly. "I was just coming back to the hall from the toilet and I saw him walk into one of the stage lights in the corridor."

Understanding dawned on Mr Bryan's face. "Oh, I see, that explains it. Oh dear."

"I did *not* walk into a light, a monster hit me on the head with a board rubber!" Anthony said, stamping his foot.

A ripple of laughter ran around the room. Even the teachers smiled.

"Yeah," called out Brett. "And I saw the Easter Bunny earlier!"

"And Doctor Who landed in the playground," said Chris.

"Come on, Anthony," Mr Bryan said in a soothing voice. "I think you'd better come to my office. I'll ring your grandfather and get him to take you home." He looked round. "Where's Miss Waters?"

"Um... Mr Bryan," Sophie put in again. "Sam and I saw her going outside."

"Outside?" Mr Bryan echoed in surprise.

Sam nodded. "She seemed to be leaving. She looked like she was in a hurry."

"Do you want me to go and have a look for her, Mr Bryan?" offered Miss Mayfield, the Class One teacher.

"Thank you, Miss Mayfield," Mr Bryan replied.

"Watch out for the monsters!" cried Anthony.

Everyone giggled as Mr Bryan hastily led Anthony away.

The supply teacher's disappearance became the talk of the school for the rest of the day. No one could work out what had happened to her, or why she had left so suddenly.

"Fancy just going off like that," Sophie heard Mrs Sheldrake, the secretary, saying to Mr Bryan at lunchtime. "No sense of responsibility."

"She seemed such a nice person too," said Mr Bryan sadly. Sophie saw him crumple up the poem he'd written, shoving it away into his trouser pocket. "I guess you never can tell with some people."

Sophie's class had their own theory about Miss Waters's disappearance.

"I reckon she got eaten by the vicious

whiteboard-rubber-throwing monster!" Jake laughed at lunchtime.

"Monsters! Argh!" said Tara, waving her arms in the air like Godzilla. "Run for your lives everyone! RUN!"

"Oooh, my name's Anthony and I'm so scared of the monsters!" said Nasim in a high-pitched voice.

Sophie's class fell about laughing.

"You know, something tells me that Anthony's going to get some pretty *monstrous* teasing when he comes back to school!" Sophie said to Sam, as they left school that day.

Sam grinned. "It serves him right for following us around."

"He might even leave us alone from now on," said Sophie. She gave a happy sigh. "Everything's worked out so well."

"I'm sorry I didn't listen to you about Miss Waters," Sam put in.

"Don't worry, I'm just glad you trusted me in the end." Sophie looked at him curiously. "Why did you?"

"I don't know." Sam frowned. "When you spoke to me, it was like a mist suddenly cleared in my head and I could think properly again.

Part of me wanted to keep believing Miss Waters was nice, but when I looked into your eyes, I just couldn't."

"Well, I'm glad," said Sophie. "I'd never have thought about using the wind turbine without you! And now all the Fog Boggarts are gone and we've only got two more gems to find."

"We'll find them!" Sam declared. Suddenly he pointed. "Look, isn't that your grandpa by the school gates?"

Sophie nodded in surprise. There was no mistaking her grandfather's trim, black-clad form. They went over. "Hi, Grandpa. What are you doing here?" she asked.

"I wanted to check you were both OK," Grandpa replied with a frown. "I knew something must be up when I heard that Anthony was talking about monsters, and Miss Waters had suddenly

left. So, what's been going on?"

"Miss Waters *was* a shadow creature," Sam said in a low voice. "Sophie was right all along."

"She was a Fog Boggart, but they can cloak themselves so the Guardian's powers don't sense them," Sophie explained. "They can control people's minds and disguise themselves too."

Grandpa groaned, clutching at his temples. "I can't believe I was fooled! I should have realised."

"You weren't the only one she tricked," Sophie reassured him. "Anyway, the important thing is she's gone now."

"And we've got the gem!" added Sam.

Grandpa looked astonished. "You've got the gem?" he echoed.

Sophie grinned. "We've got so much to tell you, Grandpa!"

Slowly, he started to smile. "It sounds like I should treat you both to an ice cream at Maggie's Café, and you can tell me everything that's been going on today. How does that sound?"

"Brilliant!" Sophie and Sam chorused.

Grandpa set off. Sophie nudged Sam as they followed him. "Pity Anthony's not here," she whispered. "I bet he'd have liked some *i-scream*."

Sam's eyes twinkled. "I don't know, maybe

we could take him back a *s-cream* cake."

"Or a plate of custard *s-creams*!" said Sophie.

Giggling together, they followed Grandpa down the sunny street.

9

In the Woods...

"NOOOOOOO!" Deep in the Shadow Woods a loud cry rang out. "It can't be true!" King Ug leapt off his tree-stump throne and marched around in a rage. "The Fog Boggarts can't have failed. You're lying!" he shouted at the three Ink Cap Goblins who were cowering before him.

"We're not, oh Great King Ug!"

"We saw it happen, Your Most Handsome Majesty!"

"Potato Nose got the key back!"

"The key!" King Ug swirled round, his cunning eyes suddenly alight. "Where is it?"

"Here, Your Great Majestical Ugness." Potato Nose held out the metal key. "The Fog Boggarts dropped it when they dissolved in the sun."

King Ug swept the key out of his hands. "The precious key!" He held it close to his chest. "It shall open the gateway yet."

"Um, King Ug…" Big Feet raised his hand cautiously. "I've got an idea of who we can ask to help us get one of the last two hidden gems."

"An idea?" King Ug looked as if Big Feet had just said he liked knitting baby blankets for a hobby. "You don't have ideas, you worm-brained fungus head!"

"Sorry, Great King Ug." Big Feet looked at the floor.

"So what are we going to do, Your Majesty?" asked Potato Nose.

King Ug marched up and down. "We will… um…" He frowned and changed direction. "Yes, let's…. um…" He scratched his flaking head. "Hmmm, we'll um…" King Ug hesitated and then strode over to Big Feet. He lowered his voice. "So, this idea of yours – what is it precisely?"

Big Feet whispered a few words into his ear. For a moment, Ug stood very still and then a smile crept across his face and he nodded. He turned to Flaky Face and Potato Nose. "I have had an idea!" he announced grandly. "We shall ask for the help of the…"

He lowered his voice and whispered two words.

Flaky Face and Potato Nose caught their breath in excitement. "Brilliant, King Ug!" whooped Flaky Face.

Potato Nose nodded. "The Guardian will never be able to stop *them!* That's a great idea!"

"It was *my* idea!" protested Big Feet. "I... ow!" He broke off as Ug tripped him over.

"Oh, I am so very clever!" Ug chortled. "This time nothing shall stop us!"

The other Ink Cap Goblins, even Big Feet, joined in with the laughter.

"We'll get the gem!"

"We'll open the gateway!"

"That Guardian won't know what's hit her!"

King Ug rubbed his hands in glee. This time, nothing but nothing could go wrong!

THE
SHADOW
FILES

Chameleon Gnomes

Skin can change to different colours depending on surroundings. Chameleon Gnomes can also disguise themselves and look like different things e.g. tree stumps.

Hard to tell the difference!

Good hearing

Good eyesight

Long and sticky

Ugly

Like Anthony!

Habitat: Chameleon Gnomes prefer to live among bramble bushes where they reach out and grab prey as it passes. *Watch feet in woods!*

Diet: Chameleon Gnomes eat frogs, toads, rabbits, squirrels.

Fighting them: Avoid tongue which is coated with poison.

Avoid their teeth, too - they look sharp!

Mist Sprites

Made of mist and so impossible to hurt or hold, Mist Imps are shy but can be mischievous. Like Chameleon Gnomes, they can change their appearance and have even been known to mist people's minds and control their thoughts.

P.T.O.

Also worth noting, although Mist Imps are unable to mist the Guardian's mind, they can cloak themselves with magic so the Guardian's powers will not detect them.

WEAPONS TO FIGHT SHADOW CREATURES

Sun

Megashooter water pistols

Starch spray

Furniture polish

Torch

Fluffy

Me!

FOG BOGGARTS

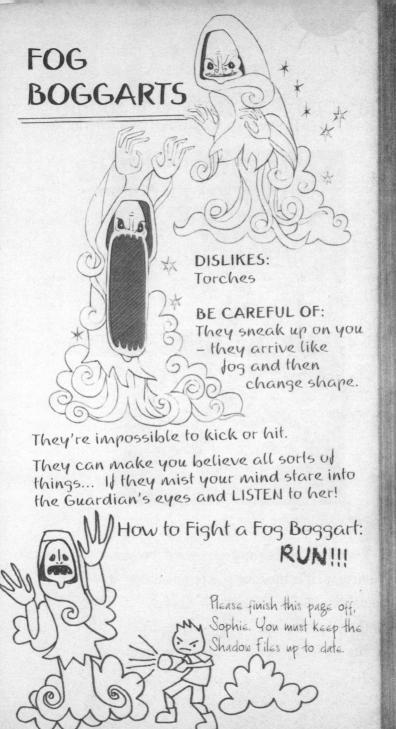

DISLIKES:
Torches

BE CAREFUL OF:
They sneak up on you – they arrive like fog and then change shape.

They're impossible to kick or hit.

They can make you believe all sorts of things... If they mist your mind stare into the Guardian's eyes and LISTEN to her!

How to Fight a Fog Boggart:
RUN!!!

Please finish this page off, Sophie. You must keep the Shadow Files up to date.

What's next in store for Sophie?

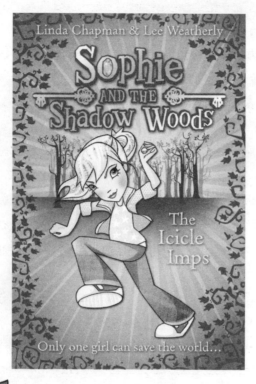

The shadow creature narrowed its eyes. "Guardian, it is time for you to be afraid," it squeaked. "Be *very* afraid."

There was a pause.

The leader looked at Sophie expectantly.

She cleared her throat. "Um, sorry," she said, spreading her hands. "But I'm kind of having problems with your general scariness. You're just so... so *cute*!"

"Cute?" the leader spat. He drew himself up to his full height of fifteen centimetres. "I warn you, we strike terror into the hearts of those who know us, Guardian!"

Sophie suppressed a laugh. "Yeah, if you're a dormouse maybe!"

"Um, Soph," Sam said uneasily as the Icicle Imps started to jump off the branches and move in around them. "They're getting quite close to us."

"So?" Sophie replied. "What are they going to do? Bite us?"

As she spoke each of the Icicle Imps drew back their lips, and a set of pointed fangs popped out of their gums – fangs that reached down their fluffy chins and looked as sharp as carving knives!

"Oh," said Sophie slowly.

"Attack!" squeaked the Icicle Imp leader.

"Run!" yelled Sam...

"Do you have what it takes to be the NEXT GUARDIAN?"

Prove your worth for a chance to win AWESOME prizes!
It's simple and fun!

Read the *Sophie and the Shadow Woods* series
Answer three questions about each book
Pass a stage, collect a gem, enter for great prizes/freebies
Pass SIX stages and get entered into the grand prize draw!

Stage Four

Answer these simple questions about *The Fog Boggarts*
1. What is the name of Sophie's headmaster?
2. Where was the blue gem hidden?
3. What did the Fog Boggart throw at Anthony?

Got the answers? Go to:
www.sophieandtheshadowwoods.com
and continue the journey!

You can find Stage One in *The Goblin King*, Stage Two in *The Swamp Boggles* and Stage Three in *The Spider Gnomes*. Look out for Stage Five in *The Icicle Imps*, out in September. Good Luck!